BEASTLY!

MONKEY MAYHEM

Andy Baxter

Illustrations by Brian Williamson

EGMONT

Special thanks to:
Nick Baker, West Jesmond Primary School,
Maney Hill Primary School
and Courthouse Junior School

EGMONT
We bring stories to life

Monkey Mayhem first published in Great Britain 2008
by Egmont UK Limited
239 Kensington High Street, London W8 6SA

Text & illustrations © 2008 Egmont UK Ltd
Text by Nick Baker
Illustrations by Brian Williamson

ISBN 978 1 4052 3938 7

1 3 5 7 9 10 8 6 4 2

A CIP catalogue record for this title is available
from the British Library

Typeset by Avon DataSet Ltd, Bidford on Avon, Warwickshire
Printed and bound in Great Britain by the CPI Group

MAX MURPHY He's ready to swing into action at any time!

Absent-minded Uncle Herbert looks after Max and his twin sister Molly during term time while their parents are away.

MOLLY MURPHY
She's ten minutes younger and ten times less hairy

Max longs for a normal family life, but that's about as likely as his uncle remembering which day of the week it is!

HERBERT SPLOTT
Uncle, brother, scatterbrain – slightly odd

Mr and Mrs Murphy are zoologists, so they're completely crazy about animals, and they're busy working on creating the best animal encyclopedia ever. Max thinks they're weird; who wants to stand around staring at sloths when you could be tucked up at home watching telly?

MR MURPHY AND MRS MURPHY
Protecting endangered species, but not always their endangered son

PROFESSOR SLYNK
His robot spies are his ears
and eyes!

And, as if all that didn't make Max's life tough
enough, his parents' sinister colleague Professor
Preston Slynk has found out his secret. Slynk's
miniature insect-robot spies are never far away . . .

They're all shapes and sizes!
Baboon males are almost twice the size of baboon females!

They have singalongs!
Baboons love to sing, and sometimes the males and females sing duets!

They're a flight risk!
Mountain gorillas are one of the most endangered species in the world. There are fewer than 650 left, which means that they could all fit on two jumbo jets with plenty of space for other passengers!

ne Facts

They're celebrities! Gorillas have attracted so much tourist attention in Rwanda that the government put pictures of them on their bank notes!

They're handy! The pigmy marmoset (a dinky little monkey) weights a tiny 130 grams and is less than 30 centimetres tall from head to tail, meaning it could easily sit in the palm of your hand!

They're loud!! Howler monkeys are so loud that their voices can be heard over a distance of several kilometres.

KENYA: The Facts

- It shares Africa's Lake Victoria with Tanzania and Uganda. It also shares Mount Kilimanjaro with Tanzania which reaches a massive 6 kilometres above sea level

- The capital is Nairobi, which is home to over 3 million people

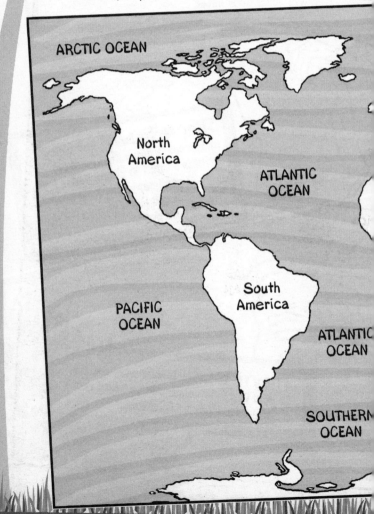

- It was formerly known as British East Africa, but became independent in 1963
- At the last count, Kenya's population was 37 million
- As well as monkeys, baboons and orang-utans, Kenya is also home to the Big Five. They are the lion, leopard, buffalo, rhinoceros and African elephant

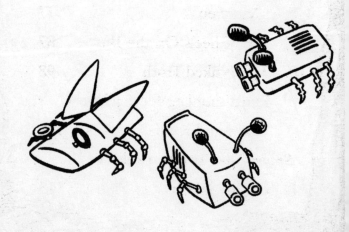

Contents

1. Crackers Christmas

'I wonder what I'm getting for Christmas this year?' Max Murphy pondered aloud, while trying to scrape the final tiny crumbs of crisp out of a monster-sized packet. 'Oh, no, I don't,' he contradicted himself. 'I already know – two weeks in a creaky old, mosquito-filled safari lodge in Kenya, being terrorised by monkeys and bats!'

'Where's your sense of adventure?' buzzed his sister Molly as she picked up bits and pieces she needed to pack, whilst dancing around to her MP3.

'It's only an hour till we leave and we have to make sure we've got everything we could possibly need.'

'It's all right for *you*,' Max said, 'but think what it could be like for me in Kenya. With my special abilities I could end up transforming into a gazelle and being eaten by a lion.'

Just then, Uncle Herbert arrived in the room on roller blades, attempted a sharp turn and collapsed into an enormous bean-bag chair.

'You're a very lucky pair!' he said, shaking his mane of yellow hair out of his eyes. 'Other children get boring old CDs and DVDs and SIBs for Christmas, but you are getting a trip to Africa! Not everyone has parents who are compiling the ultimate animal encyclopedia.'

'That's true,' Molly grinned at Max, then swung back to Uncle Herbert. 'What on earth are SIBs?'

'Straight-In-the-Bins!' grinned her uncle. Max frowned. He was still wondering how much Uncle Herbert had overheard. Max and Molly had no plans to share the secret of his ability to transform into animals with any grown-ups as yet. Not until adults — as a species — had shown any sign they could be trusted.

'So we both think Max should stop moaning,' Molly agreed. She looked at the icy rain trickling down the window. It was nearly eleven and the sun didn't seem to have bothered to rise today. Kenya was definitely a much better place to be.

'Oh, I'm not suggesting he should stop moaning,' Uncle Herbert replied with a twinkle in his eye. 'I don't think children should ever be deprived of their favourite pastimes, it's bad for their development! Now who wants to stir the anchovies into the Christmas pudding with me? If we do that today it should be delicious round about, um . . . Easter!'

Max checked he had put all his favourite games and comics in his case for the fifth time.

'You almost seem glad to get rid of us,' Max sulked, resenting his uncle's cheery mood.

'I am working on a new book of puzzles at the moment,' he said. 'Pyramid puzzles. You build up triangles of hieroglyphics and if you get the answer wrong the curse of the pharaoh falls upon you. It's great fun!'

Max grinned. Uncle Herbert was getting kookier by the day. Maybe it was worth going to Kenya just to escape from whatever bizarre Christmas lunch he was planning to serve up. Last year's snowman-shaped cauliflower cheese with chocolate sauce had been disgusting.

It wasn't long before they were rushing through the lunchtime traffic to the airport, listening to the screeching of tyres, the furious honking of horns and the angry screams of pedestrians that always accompanied their uncle's driving.

'It's very tiring being given a lift by Uncle Herbert,' Max said as the pair boarded their flight for Africa. 'I always get arm-ache keeping my hands over my eyes.'

In contrast, their flight was wonderfully smooth, with spectacular views of beautiful cloudscapes, a funny movie and even tasty food.

'You know,' ventured Molly carefully, 'Kenya might not be as bad as you think.' She was treading dangerous ground, trying to get Max to admit that he might just be wrong.

'Maybe!' Max agreed, snuggling up in his inflatable neck-supporter and trying to grab a snooze. 'Maybe in Kenya cheeseburgers grow on trees and sisters stop nattering once in a while.'

Molly jabbed her elbow hard into Max's side.

'Not bad,' said Max, as they walked up the wooden steps of the Kilimanjaro Experience Lodge. 'Only a three-hour, bumpy bus-ride from the airport – I must be getting used to this globe-trotting lark.'

'Well you're in Amboseli National Park now,' replied Molly. 'So be careful which animals you look at, or you might be doing a different kind of trotting!'

They stepped from the bright sunshine into the shade of the lodge reception. There, among the elephant sculptures and tribal masks that were decorated with plastic holly, tinsel and fake snow – a welcoming committee awaited them. It included Mum, Dad and . . . Professor Preston Slynk! Slynk's pudgy body, squeezed into a crisp new safari suit, was leaning over the reception desk. Max went white, dropped his case and almost fainted.

'Wonderful to see you two!' Mrs Murphy said,

attempting to hug her offspring. 'What on earth is the matter with Max?'

Max pointed at Slynk, who was filling his name in at the desk. 'What is HE doing here?' Max blurted.

'Quite a spot of luck,' said their father. 'We just bumped into our old chum while on baboon-watch a few days ago. When he heard you two were joining us shortly, he said he simply must see you!'

The twins exchanged a grim look. Was there no escape from their arch-enemy?

'Slynk's the name,' the smarmy scientist was saying to the receptionist. 'It's spellt like "sly" but rhymes with "wink"!' He gave a wink as he said this, which made Molly feel sick.

'Rhymes with "stink", he means!' she muttered.

Slynk waddled over to join them. With his smooth, pink skin, tiny eyes and fine black hair he reminded Molly of an overgrown baby.

'At last!' Slynk gushed with pretend joy at seeing Max. 'It's been so long! You children have grown so much since the last time I saw you. Max has positively *transformed*!' he grinned, stressing the last word deliberately.

Same old Slynk, Max thought, gloomily.

'Let me show you your room,' said Mrs Murphy. 'There was rather a fine *phasmatodea* – that's stick insect – in my shower this morning. Perhaps you'll be lucky enough to have one too!'

While Mr and Mrs Murphy were looking the other way, Slynk glared at Max and Molly. Max's blood ran cold. The man was pure evil.

After a night's sleep, disturbed only by the whine of mosquitoes and the rooftop antics of black-faced monkeys, the twins were having a buffet-style breakfast on the shady veranda of the lodge, enjoying the breathtaking view of Mount Kilimanjaro.

'An all-you-can-eat buffet really wasn't meant for people like you, Max,' his mum sighed. 'Please leave some food for the rest of the guests!'

'We are so lucky to have reservations here!' Mr Murphy said. 'Amboseli National Park is three-hundred-and-ninety square kilometres of animal-watching heaven! There are over sixty major species here, including the fascinating yellow baboon!'

'Talking of baboons . . .' said Max, nodding towards Slynk, who was leaning on the veranda nearby, glancing around shiftily as if waiting for someone.

'Why has he got that enormous bag with him?' asked Molly. Her mum smiled.

'Surely it's obvious. Preston has very sensibly prepared an extensive first-aid kit. Medicines, syringes, forceps, sterilising equipment – as well as all the latest gadgets for monitoring brain waves and taking blood samples . . .'

Max kicked Molly under the table.

'That stuff is all to use on *me*!' he hissed at her. Their parents started to pore over a map, but Max kept watching Slynk. Two local men with sun hats pulled right down over their eyes came up to shake hands with him. Slynk swiftly handed over some bank-notes and waved them away.

'Professor Stink is *definitely* up to something!' Max whispered to Molly. 'We can't take our eyes off him for an instant!'

2. Stop Bugging Me

'Great news, kids!' announced Mrs Murphy excitedly. 'First thing tomorrow we're off on safari! Hiking in the shadow of Kilimanjaro ... campfires and sizzling bacon ... sleeping under the stars with a birdsong lullaby. It'll be the experience of a lifetime! What a way to spend Christmas Eve.'

Max rolled his yes. *Oh, no!* he thought. *Not another 'experience of a lifetime'.*

'It'll be much more fun than sitting at home scoffing sweets and watching TV!' continued Mum.

No, it won't! Max wanted to shout, thinking chocolate and television was the perfect holiday combination, not to mention wrapping presents and decorating the Christmas tree. But he bit his tongue.

'Go and pack your things. Then we'll meet the rest of the party.'

'Party?' said Max. 'Anyone would think it was Christmas!'

Max and Molly were the last to arrive in the lounge. Mum and Dad were already there, together with a dozen other safari-goers and their guide, Mr Ongondo. He stood by a massive fireplace, above which hung the mouldy head of a very dead buffalo.

'Welcome, travellers,' he said, and he pointed at the buffalo's head. 'This poor glass-eyed creature reminds us why we're here – to see our wildlife in its natural state, not stuffed full of sawdust.'

'Sawdust and glass eyes sound brilliant if you ask me,' whispered Max to Molly. 'Live animals are dangerous!'

'You'll be quite safe,' continued Mr Ongondo, 'if you follow the rules. So listen carefully, especially you two children. We don't usually allow youngsters on these trips, but your Mum and Dad tell me you're experienced travellers, so we've made an exception.'

Mr Ongondo started to list the rules: 'Number one,' he announced, 'and this is the most important rule of all: out in the bush we all stick together, *always*.' Max yawned. He was starting to feel as glassy-eyed as the stuffed buffalo's head, and his thoughts wandered.

Eventually he heard Mr Ongondo say, 'Now let's introduce ourselves,' and a hubbub of voices filled the room. Thinking a read of his comic would be much more fun than yacking to boring grown-ups, Max crept away. He had almost reached the door when something damp and podgy grabbed his shoulder.

'Going somewhere?' Max gasped. It was Slynk, shoving him roughly back into the lounge.

'Wait here, boy,' he ordered in a menacing growl, 'or there'll be trouble.' Then he called out, 'Mr Ongondo, may I propose we drink a toast to happy travellers?'

'A marvellous idea, Professor,' said Mr Ongondo. 'Everyone . . . get yourself a drink.'

Slynk was first to the bar and grabbed a glass of juice. Nervously, he dropped a tiny green tablet in it and strolled back to Max.

'Here,' Slynk said, thrusting the glass into Max's hand, 'thought I'd save you the trouble.'

Max peered at it. It looked like pea soup from

a health-food shop, but at least it was fizzy. He lifted the glass to take a glug but Molly grabbed his arm. 'No!' she whispered. 'I saw Stink drop something in it. I think it's drugged!'

'Phew! Thanks, Molly,' said Max. 'You saved my bacon.'

'You know we'll have to tell Mum and Dad about it now,' said Molly. 'Drugging you could've been really dangerous.'

'No! We can't. We agreed, remember. If they find out about my transformations, they'll *never* let me out of their sight again. I won't even be able to go to the toilet without them waiting by the door in case I turn into a fish.'

'In that case,' said Molly, 'I reckon Stink needs teaching a lesson ... and some of his own medicine should do the trick.' They waited till Slynk was chatting to their parents, then went into action.

'Hello, Professor,' said Max, smiling innocently

and holding out the drugged drink. 'Sorry to interrupt, but you left your drink over there.'

Mr and Mrs Murphy beamed proudly at their well-mannered children. Slynk couldn't make a fuss in public, so he scowled and took the glass.

Max and Molly watched closely, but he didn't take a sip.

'Aren't you going to drink it, Professor?' Molly asked sweetly. 'After all, we brought it over specially.'

'Yes, of course,' he replied irritably. 'All in good time.' Then, just as Mr Ongondo walked past, he faked a nudge and dropped the glass on the floor.

'Dear me! Now I need another one. Would you mind, Max?' He leaned close and hissed viciously, 'Listen to me, boy! I've got you this time. Out in the wild there's a long way to run but no place to hide, so don't try anything stupid.' Then, slapping Max on the back as though they were the best of friends, he added a loud and cheery, 'Ha, ha, ha, that's terrific, Max. Just great.'

Next morning, with the sun shimmering on the horizon, they set off into the savannah. Until they left the lodge, Slynk had stuck to Max and Molly like a limpet, but now he led the way with Mr Ongondo, leaving the twins dawdling at the back. Molly smelled something fishy . . . and it wasn't the salmon-paste sandwiches in her packed lunch!

After half-an-hour's hiking, their parents

dropped back and joined them. 'Isn't this great!' Mum said cheerfully. 'Shall we play a game?'

'How about I-spy?' said Max miserably.

Already his legs ached, his feet had blisters and he felt so hungry he could eat a ton of chocolate. 'I-spy with my little eye a million miles of dry grass and a mountain. Oh, I want a rest!' he said, and he sat down on a rock.

Mr Murphy suddenly dashed into the bushes and a moment later rushed back exclaiming, 'Did you see that? I'm sure it was *grammomys gigas*!'

'A giant thicket rat?' said Mum, equally excited. 'Wow! They're rare.'

'Talking of rats,' Molly whispered to Max, 'Stink's up to something, but I can't put my finger on it.'

Max rubbed his sore legs. 'I'm just glad he's leaving me alone for once. The way he follows me around really bugs me.'

'Bugs!' cried Molly. 'That's it!' She began frantically emptying her rucksack. Max looked puzzled, until he saw crawling over Molly's spare socks a tiny metal box with blinking red eyes, eight metal legs and a wobbly antenna.

'A robot spider spy!' Molly whispered. She pointed at Max's pack and he tipped everything out too. He looked sheepish when five bags of chocolate buttons fell from his rolled-up pyjamas.

'There! It's on your torch!'

'Let's smash 'em,' said Max.

'Better still,' said Molly giggling, 'leave them under this rock and Slynk can bug some real bugs!'

They had just stopped for a drink when Slynk started a frenzied war dance, hopping round madly and pulling his trousers off.

'Don't look, Molly!' called Mrs Murphy.

'Help! Get it off!' yelled Slynk, scrabbling backwards as a massive hairy tarantula crawled from his discarded trousers, up his legs and on to his baggy Y-fronts.

Calmly, Mr Murphy picked it up and dropped it in a bush.

'I was just researching the effect of human movement on spiders,' said Slynk, putting on some shorts so nothing else could climb up his trouser leg. 'Really, I'm not at all afraid of the dear little creatures.'

'Not mechanical ones, anyway,' muttered Max. Slynk scowled.

They had just packed their flasks ready to move on, when the ugliest pig Molly had ever seen crashed through the undergrowth and ran towards the Professor.

'Slynk!' shouted Mr Murphy.

'No, it's a warthog,' Max chuckled as it ran off.

'It's much better looking!'

They walked on and the sun burned hotter and hotter. Mr Ongondo pointed out wildebeest, hyenas and gazelles. 'Did you know,' he said when they spotted a herd of elephants splashing in a swamp, 'that we have more than a thousand elephants in this reserve?'

Max looked longingly at them. *If only I could change into an elephant,* he dreamed, *I could have a cool shower . . . and Stink wouldn't stand a chance!* He stared at the elephants for ages, but they didn't even look up. Perhaps on this holiday he wouldn't change after all.

Max woke from his daydream to see Mr Ongondo pointing at a clump of trees. 'If you look over there,' he was saying, 'you can see a family of yellow baboons. Interesting creatures; they have pouched cheeks, like hamsters, in which they store food to eat later.'

'Like Max's rucksack you mean?' said Molly laughing, but Max didn't react. She looked across and saw him grimace.

He hadn't heard a word. His watering eyes were locked in a stare with the chief baboon. A familiar electric shock fizzled all the way down his spine, his mouth tasted of mouldy muesli and his heart thumped like a lorry engine. Sweat trickled down his forehead and he retched as though he was about to vomit.

Molly recognised that look. 'Max!' she whispered, shaking him. 'It's happening again! Quick, run for those trees!'

3. The Max Factor

'**O**h!' groaned Max, his eyes stinging as though he had pepper in them. Groggy and half-blinded by tears, he could hear a voice calling, like an echo, down a long tunnel. 'Hurry!'

Molly? he thought, shaking his head to clear his mind.

'You've got to go!' Molly whispered desperately. 'Now! Before anyone sees you.'

'OK,' he mumbled. He tried to stand, but his bones felt as soft and rubbery as cheesy strings.

Fortunately, the rest of the safari party was watching Professor Slynk. With his shorts on, the bare skin of his pale legs acted like a flea magnet. Every tick and midge in the savannah jumped at the chance to chomp his marshmallow-soft flesh, which was now a mass of scarlet bumps. Slynk grumbled and rubbed soothing cream into his stinging skin, as everyone in the party crowded round offering advice.

Max took his chance and stumbled into the bushes, flinging off his clothes as he went. He squirmed and scratched as an unbearable itching spread across his belly, down his legs and all the way up his back. 'Eeearg!' he shrieked as he peeled off his sweaty socks, and a mat of bristly hair burst from every pore of his skin. Rippling muscles bulged from his dangling arms, stretching like strings of warm treacle until his knuckles dragged on the ground.

'Yow!' he yelped, as his face exploded from inside and four great fangs sliced through his gums.

'Noooo,' he whined, as his nose and mouth puffed into a smooth black snout and his eyes sucked deep into his brows.

As he tried to stand up, a long tail whiplashed

from his bottom. It waved about like a furry walking stick and he toppled forward on to all fours.

A secretary bird in the high tree tops tipped its head to one side, staring quizzically at the boy who was now a yellow baboon.

Max chortled as a delicious joy welled up inside him and grew into howls of uncontrollable laughter. He jumped up and down, turned cartwheels and chased his tail, enjoying the thrill of restless, boundless energy. He leapt into the trees, swinging from branch to branch on his long hairy arms.

Just below him stood Molly, staring anxiously at the bushes. He reached down and knocked off her hat.

'Eeeek,' she squealed, and Max-the-baboon nearly fell out of the tree laughing.

Molly stepped back in fright, but quickly

recognised Max's bright blue eyes and winked – at exactly the wrong moment! Alerted by Molly's squeal, Slynk had looked up from treating his spotty legs, and spotted them!

'I'll have you!' he growled through clenched teeth.

'What's that Professor?' asked Mrs Murphy brightly.

'Er . . . I was dreaming of dinner,' said Slynk quickly. 'I must have said, "I'll have stew."'

As the safari trekked slowly on, Max moved alongside it, hidden among the trees. He had so much energy he just wanted to race about and play! It drove him mad.

He tried to stay near his human family, but longed for company and fun. Wonderful scents wafted on the wind, the tantalising smells flashed into his mind as pictures of luscious fruits or crunchy beetles.

A troop of young baboons was playing rough-and-tumble nearby. Thrilled, Max raced to join in, but just as he reached them, a fierce bark rang out and they scampered off. He followed, but they backed away every time he got close, which made him feel even more lonely.

Thunder rumbled and he looked around for signs of a storm coming. Then from very close it came again, and he realised the rumble was his belly complaining – he hadn't eaten since breakfast.

Some baboons were foraging for food and Max copied them; pulling seeds from tufts of grass and picking wriggling, juicy grubs from lumps of old elephant poo. He found a luscious-looking maggot as fat as his finger and lifted it to his drooling mouth. *Oooh! It would be heaven to bite off its head and squish it between his teeth . . . and to suck out all the sweet juices, and . . .* he jerked back as the voice

of Max-the-boy inside his head yelled, *No! Stop!* Just in time he flicked it away.

The rumbling in his belly didn't stop though. The baboons were now munching spiky leaves from a weed that grew everywhere. Max remembered his dad calling it devil's thorn. It looked about as nice as it sounded and after the close shave with the maggot he left it alone.

The baboons moved into the shade of an acacia wood. Max followed, watching as they picked up pods that fell from the trees and cracked them open with their teeth. Max tried it and inside each one found seeds like tiny black fleas. He popped one in his mouth and chuckled as the mustardy taste tickled his nose. Yum! He rushed round happily scoffing hundreds but eventually gave up – he'd never fill up on these tiny things. Worse still, his nose was almost fizzing and needed an urgent pick! He turned his back so no one could see and put his finger up one nostril. *Brilliant! A perfect fit.*

'Ugh!' he cried, yanking out his finger and rubbing his snout with the back of his hand. The finger stank of elephant poo!

Being careful not to squash his new tail, Max sat down. He felt horribly thirsty after eating all those acacia seeds and cross with the baboons who wouldn't let him play.

Looking round he saw a smudge on the horizon. Thinking it might be a lake he raced off for a drink. He bounded along on all fours, shrieking and chattering with joy, happily imagining the first refreshing slurp. After running for ages he looked up and saw the smudge was moving slowly . . . towards *him*! It looked like a giant millipede growing gradually larger until it broke into a hundred pieces, each with four legs, a great muscled body and a huge horned head.

Max realised they were caped buffalo, just like the one at the lodge . . . except for the sawdust and glass eyes.

What did Dad say about them? thought Max. *I think it was something like, 'They're bad tempered and dangerous, and you should never annoy them'.*

One huge buffalo lowered its head and took a plodding step forwards. It looked so slow and clumsy Max wasn't afraid – it'd be easy to outrun a big lump like that!

Dad would tell him to back away slowly, thought Max. *But, poor things, they must be sooo bored just munching grass. I bet they'd like some fun!* And though he knew he should leave them alone, Max couldn't help himself, he frolicked around clapping and whooping. Then he danced a jig, stuck out his tongue and took a bow. He tried to salute but he fell over backwards, then rolled around giggling. Though his sides ached from laughing, he lifted one arm and screeching, 'Eeeee, eeeee', put his thumb on his nose and wiggled his fingers. Then he heard more thunder, but this time it definitely was not from his belly – the ground trembled and a great cloud of dust rose from the hundreds of stomping hooves heading for him at high speed . . . He'd started a stampede!

4. Game For a Laugh

Max tried to yell for help, but no sound came out. Searching frantically for an escape he saw only one hope – a forest 200 metres away. With his heart thumping and legs shaking, he ran. It was just like doing the Wellington boot race at school, though he'd never had a hundred buffalo charging after him on sports day!

'Mum ... Dad ... Molly!' he cried, certain that any minute he'd be pounded into the ground. Then suddenly he wasn't thinking but bounding along. Every leaf and blade of grass seemed clear and sharp. Carried by instinct, the ground flew by as a blur below his feet, the wind rippled through his fur. *Not far now . . . a few metres more*, he felt snorting hot breath on his back. *Almost . . . there!* With a final leap Max grabbed a branch and swung up safe above the thrashing horns.

Chuckling with relief, he hung upside down and beat his hands on his chest. He longed, now he was safe, to poke fun at the slowcoach old buffalo who couldn't catch him!

He didn't though. *I'm not actually king of the jungle,* he thought. *I'm not even king of the savannah.* What had Mr Ongondo said about the yellow baboon's predators? He wished he'd listened. Leopards, lions, hyenas and there were probably loads of others. *What if I meet one of them?* thought Max.

As the buffalo wandered off, Max sat in the tree wondering where he was and if he would ever find his family again – and what about Christmas? No, he didn't want to think about that. He dropped to the ground and sniffed the air, hoping for a clue. Suddenly something enormous came crashing through the undergrowth. Without thinking he screeched and faced the noise, mouth wide open, lips drawn back to reveal his great fangs. *That should scare it away*, he thought. *Whatever it was*. Peering through the twigs and leaves, he saw four tall poles. *Stink! It's Stink on stilts, trying to catch me from the tree tops!* He looked up and there, instead of Slynk, was the head of a giraffe batting its eyelashes in surprise. Max let out a grunt of relief, and his expression relaxed into a rather embarrassed grin.

Desperately thirsty and with no idea which way to go, he set off looking for anything bright green that might mean there was water nearby. Lizards scuttled from rocks and birds clattered from the undergrowth as he bounded along. Once he followed the bed of a dried-out stream and found a beautiful pool. He rushed towards the bank and almost ran into a menacing black rhino. He stopped just in time and backed away . . . after the buffalo he wasn't taking any chances.

A little later, a banded groundling dragonfly zipped by. The dark brown stripes on its wings blurred in the sunlight. Knowing they lived near water, Max skipped after it. He followed the dragonfly, but it kept following him and he wasted ten minutes going round in circles. He moved on thinking, *How hard can it be to find a drink out here?*

Suddenly a hare shot across the path. Instantly, uncontrollably, Max was chasing, skipping, dashing, leaping, swiping at the hare as it flashed by one side, clutching air as it zipped by the other. He could smell its terror, feel its desperation to escape, but that only added to the exhilaration of the chase! His fingertips brushed the hare's ears and he lunged forward just as it jigged the other away, and Max lost his balance, tumbling and rolling over and over as the hare skittered to freedom. He lay down, laughing and panting and dizzy, until the sparks stopped flashing in his eyes and the blood stopped whooshing round inside his head, wondering what he would have done if he had caught it. Half of him was enjoying the thought of sinking his teeth into the hare's neck, ripping the skin off its back and feasting on the moist pink flesh inside . . . while the other half was thinking it would have made a nice pet for Molly.

Just then, Max's ears pricked up. He could hear laughter and twitched nervously, unsure whether he felt happy or afraid. *Is that Dad chuckling at one of his own feeble jokes?* he thought. *Or is it Slynk planning some evil scheme to catch me?* Cautiously, he lifted his head, and peered over the tall grass.

'Ay-eek! Ay-eek!' he screeched, instantly terrified and angry as a red mist filled his eyes. He had never felt so cross and he beat the ground, baring his teeth at the vicious, murderous laughing hyena! Knowing it would stop at nothing to kill him, Max went wild, kicking up a terrible commotion, growling, spitting and waving his arms . . . until the hyena ran away!

'Rishhh,' hissed Max after it, and he did a little victory dance. He felt so proud: he had seen off one

of the most dangerous predators on the savannah! *Wait till I tell Molly!* he thought, walking away with a swagger. But suddenly he froze. Sniffing at the grass where he had followed the dragonfly, a lioness prowled – the lioness that had scared off the hyena!

She'd be hunting for food for her cubs. And being torn to shreds as lunch for some giant kittens was not top of Max's things-to-do-this-holiday list. Watching her the whole time, he very slowly and very quietly backed away, taking care not to trip on a stone or snap a twig. After five minutes he made it to the safety of a clump of bushes, where he found a pool filled by a bubbling spring. He gave himself a pat on the back - an easy task with his long arms. Then he sucked up mouthfuls of ice-cold water that tasted better than any cola he'd ever drunk in his life.

Feeling refreshed, Max wanted to play again and started pulling faces at his reflection in the pool. He stretched his lips and wobbled his cheeks. It was the funniest thing he'd seen in ages. He really wanted to laugh, but he couldn't – the lioness might still be close enough to hear, and just that thought made Max tremble.

Shadows passed over the pool and Max looked up. High above circled a wake of vultures. Mum had said they could tell an animal was about to die and flew round like guests at a funeral before swooping down to feast on the carcass.

Max gulped, hoping they were not looking at him. Across the pool something grunted. He tensed, ready to scream or fight or run. Then came a gurgling squeal and Max saw a warthog piglet stuck in a hole. Its mother was running to and fro snorting, nudging its baby, but the piglet couldn't escape.

He looked back across the savannah. The lioness had pricked up her ears, listening to the

squeals. Instinct told him to run away, but Max-the-boy wanted to help the piglet. He looked again towards the lioness . . . she was creeping his way. *Run! Run! Run for your life!* Max-the-baboon told him, and though in his head he wanted to help the piglet, Max crept away. *But the poor piglet!* thought Max-the-boy. *I can't leave it to die. I must help it, I must!*

5. I'm a Celebrity – Get Me Out of Here!

Fighting the instinct to save himself, Max raced to the far side of the pool. He reached into the hole and grabbed the piglet's legs, which kicked so ferociously he could hardly hold on. He tugged and yanked, but the little creature was wedged tight, and the harder he pulled, the louder the piglet squealed. Not knowing that Max was trying to help, the mother began snorting, stamping her feet and lowering her head to attack.

I'm only trying to help! Max wanted to say, but all

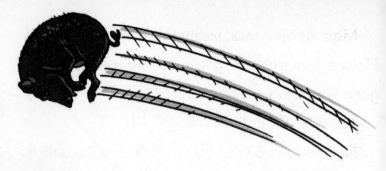

that came out were screeches and barks.

Why did I bother? he wondered, certain that any second now the lioness would attack. He put his feet either side of the hole and gave one gigantic heave. With a final squeal the piglet flew out and landed, wriggling and kicking, in the dust. Then it jumped up as if nothing had happened and trotted off to join its mother. The mother looked at Max, and he liked to think she gave him a grateful smile before running off, leaving Max to face the lioness alone, which seemed most ungrateful, come to think of it.

He scanned the grassland for the lioness, but now the squealing had stopped she had lost interest and wandered away.

Max sat on a rock, resting his head in his hands. He was just wondering which way his family had gone when he heard a voice.

Mum? he thought.

He had scanned the area twice before he noticed a movement behind a bush. Hidden near the track stood a blonde woman wearing a safari jacket and gabbling excitedly into a microphone. Beside her, a

man with a camera was filming Max's every move!

'Unbelievable! Did you get that, Bill?' she yelled at the cameraman. 'The bit where he pulled the legs? I've never seen anything like it! Just wait till the studio gets this. I'll be ... sorry, *we'll* be famous!'

Brilliant! thought Max, *I'm on TV! I'll be a celebrity! I might even get my own show* – Piglet Rescue. He chuckled to himself and was about to take a bow when he realised the danger. If this got out he'd have herds of wildlife reporters and swarms of Slynks after him.

How much had they filmed already? If they managed to link those tapes to him, he'd be in big trouble. He had no choice. He *had* to steal that film!

First though, he needed to stop them filming. He began acting exactly like a normal baboon, chewing seeds from acacia pods, scratching his belly and picking fleas from his fur, though he couldn't bring himself to eat them as the real baboons did.

After a while, the film crew packed up, jumped into their safari truck and were jolted off over the dusty track, back towards the herd of buffalo and the troop of baboons Max had seen earlier.

As soon as they set off, Max gave chase. Following the truck was the easy bit – the crew couldn't see him racing along in their dust trail. The problem was how to grab the film when they stopped. He'd have to distract them.

The camera truck pulled off the road. While the crew was busy preparing their equipment, Max had an idea. *Maybe I can get the baboons to help.* Although they hadn't let him join them that morning, they'd be afraid of the humans in the truck and might now welcome him as one of their kind.

He moved towards them, but immediately barks rang out and they backed away. How did they know he was different? Was it his smell? He sniffed under his arms and wrinkled his nose. Oh . . .

He got as close as they would allow and tried acting out his plan. He pointed at the truck and turned an invisible steering wheel. Then he pretended to grab the camera and run away. Then he jumped up and down on the imaginary camera. Simple! An idiot could follow that.

The baboons looked puzzled and frightened – they had no idea what this weird, smelly, blue-eyed intruder was doing waving his arms around and behaving so strangely.

It's so obvious! thought Max. *You must understand!* . . . but they didn't get it at all.

Struggling to control his frustration, Max tried again, but the harder he tried the more desperate he became and the wilder he looked. The young baboons ran to their mothers, while the males curled their lips and bared their teeth.

Max told himself to calm down and start from the beginning. He took a deep breath, put one finger on his arm and nodded. Then he put three fingers on his other arm and nodded. Then he drew a box in the air and started turning an invisible handle on the side. He'd played this game last Christmas.

Then came the presenter's voice again, shouting hysterically, 'You're watching Katie Plank reporting from the Amboseli National Park in Kenya. This afternoon we have witnessed the most astonishing event in the history of zoology. We have discovered a baboon displaying advanced human behaviour. It's been acting in a way that would be remarkable even in a human child of nursery age.'

Oi! thought Max. *I'm at high school!*

'I'm not suggesting that this is true intelligence,' continued the presenter. 'It is after all a dumb animal.'

Angrily, Max turned to face the presenter with his hands on his hips. *Who're you calling a dumb animal?* he said, but all Katie Plank heard was 'Grrr, ugh, raar'.

'Sure you're getting this, Bill?' Katie shrieked. 'It's priceless!'

This is getting worse, thought Max, realising that he was no nearer persuading the baboons to help him, and now the crew had even more incriminating film.

He couldn't attack the camera crew alone, but how else could he make the baboons understand? *Perhaps if I crawl towards them flat on my belly with my hands on my head, like someone approaching a king,* he thought, *they'll see I'm no threat.*

So, with nothing to lose but his dignity, Max lay in the dirt. With his bottom in the air and his tail up like a bent periscope, he shuffled forwards. After a few metres he looked up to see how he was doing. The females and youngsters were huddled together in terror, while the males were leaping

about and screeching more frantically than ever.

He looked round at the camera crew. They had their camera pointed right behind him. *The shame! If I don't get that tape, my bottom will star in every wildlife documentary in the world.*

Max crawled on further and checked again.

'Uggr, uggr, unk!' he cried. He had tried to say, *No, don't run away!* because now the whole troop was fleeing, running at top speed towards the wooded slopes of Mount Kilimanjaro. Max raced after them, waving and crying out in the friendliest manner he could imagine, but they wouldn't stop.

Then, above the noise of his panting breath and the swishing of dry grass on his feet, came a low throaty roar. A prickle of terror fizzed down his spine, all the way to the tip of his tail. Max stopped mid bound . . . turned oh-so-slowly around . . . and there, about to spring, crouched a snarling, cold-eyed leopard.

6. A Bit Cagey

Max bared his teeth as viciously as he knew how and eyed the leopard. It growled back, strong, agile . . . and not at all impressed by his attitude.

Again, the angry red mist flowed into Max's eyes, but this time he concentrated hard to clear the fog. Against the buffalo, instinct had saved him, but against the leopard he had to keep control. His animal self would either flee or fight, but he knew he couldn't outrun the leopard for long, or win a battle. There was only one way he could beat the leopard: he had to out-think it.

Max checked he was heading the right way. He knew he wouldn't get a second chance. 'Eeeeeek!' he shrieked. The leopard stopped in its tracks just long enough for Max to turn and run.

In seconds, the leopard recovered and was swiping and snapping, breathing down his neck. Max bounded over fallen logs and crashed through bushes that ripped his fur and scratched his feet. He tripped on an ant-hill and tumbled over and over. A searing pain shot through his tail as a slicing claw tore through fur and skin, gashing him to the bone. He choked back a scream and kicked out, smacking the leopard in the face. It fell back stunned and Max raced on, legs aching, sweat dripping from his eyebrows. Moments later the leopard was back, angrier than ever, snarling and pouncing as Max jiggled and

twisted like the hare that had eluded him earlier. Panting . . . breathless . . . Max knew he couldn't last much longer. He looked up and screeched: he had run straight back towards the buffalo . . . Exactly as planned.

He shot towards the herd howling and screaming, starting another stampede. Hundreds of buffalo charged again, right at him . . . and the leopard. Briefly, Max let the animal in him take over. As the breath of the first thundering beast huffed in his face he strained every muscle, leapt right over its head and landed smack on its back. It bucked like a rodeo bull but he sprang to the next buffalo, riding backwards and bareback like a circus acrobat. Jerking and twisting it tried to throw him off, but Max's supple legs rode every jolt. Max-the-boy took control again. *Fantastic! This is just like Logjam Rapids*, he thought, imagining himself playing his friend Jake's computer game, jumping from log to log across a raging river. *It's on my Christmas list*, he thought briefly. *I wonder if I've got it.* But this was no time to daydream. If he fell now it would be for real, into a deadly sea of stamping hooves. Onwards he hopped from back to back, all the way through the herd until, with a final vault, he landed safely on the ground. There he scanned the flattened grass for that speckled coat and those hungry eyes. All clear. The leopard had gone.

Brilliant! Max thought, punching the air in celebration, then he remembered the film crew. They might be watching him right now! The gash in his tail hurt like a finger slammed in a door and he felt exhausted. Worse still, despite all the trouble with the leopard, he was no nearer to getting that film. He couldn't give up, though. He *had* to get it back.

Max turned towards the safari truck, hoping the baboons hadn't run too far. He needed their help: he couldn't do it alone.

Hiding in long grass, enjoying the chirruping of larks high above the savannah, he listened for the voice of Katie Plank. All quiet. He peered between the dry stems. *No! They've gone!*

The safari truck had left. In its place stood a lorry piled high with wire cages. *Perhaps the park rangers are releasing some new animals*, he thought, still busy searching for the film crew. They were nowhere in sight.

Max realised he needed a new plan. Whenever he moved it attracted the attention of some predator determined to have him for lunch. If life were this dangerous as a baboon, he wouldn't stand a chance if he changed back to Max now. Perhaps, he wondered, he could hitch a ride with these rangers?

Just then the lorry doors opened and out jumped two men. Max recognised them at once. They were not rangers at all, but the two men who had met Slynk on the veranda! They were still wearing their sun hats pulled down over their eyes.

One of them had a walkie-talkie pressed to his ear and was shouting into the mouthpiece. Max was too far away to hear clearly, but a few words carried to him on the breeze. 'Found them . . . no, can't . . . wilco, Professor . . . over and out.'

Professor! Who else can it be but Slynk's henchmen? thought Max, as he watched the men unload cages from the back of the lorry. Then each grabbed a net from a wooden trunk.

Max shook in terror. Why hadn't he guessed? Slynk was probably tracking him with a robot bug, as usual. He crouched, ready to flee, expecting the men to chase him, but instead they carried their nets round the other side of the lorry.

'Eeek! Eeek!' came a shriek and Max watched, horrified, as Slynk's thugs netted a baboon and threw it roughly into one of the cages, beating it back with sticks until they managed to slam the door shut and click on a padlock.

Max slapped his back and groaned in agitation. What were they doing to the poor creature? Why were they being so cruel? They came back with another and another, forcing them into the cages and snapping on locks until nearly all the cages were full.

The baboons that were still free didn't seem to know what to do. Some screeched and jumped up and down angrily. Others started to run away, then stopped. They were totally confused. Perhaps their leader was among the prisoners?

The man with the walkie-talkie called again, pointing at the few baboons that were still free while he talked. 'Yes, Professor . . . all of them? OK. Over and out.' The men went back to work to round up the stragglers and Max smacked his forehead – he had figured out Slynk's plan.

Slynk hadn't bugged him after all. Instead, his bully boys were rounding up every baboon they could find; hoping one of them would be him!

Over by the lorry the trapped baboons were screaming and rattling their cages. The half-dozen that were still free started to run, but Max knew they'd be caught before long. What terrible things would Slynk do to them before he realised he hadn't managed to catch Max?

Max felt guilty and desperate. It was all his fault! If he hadn't knocked Molly's hat off, Slynk wouldn't have seen him, and if Slynk hadn't seen him these thugs wouldn't be catching the poor baboons. Maybe the troop hadn't welcomed him, but Max was sure they'd hate being trapped.

He didn't know what to do first. By now, Mum and Dad would be frantic with worry, so should he let Molly know he was OK? Should he get that tape from the film crew before they went home? Or should he help the trapped baboons?

Then a terrible wail came from a baboon struggling in a tangled net and Max knew right then that he couldn't leave. Even if it meant risking capture by Professor Slynk, he had to save the troop!

7. Animal Rescue

'**O**h, my poor baby!' wailed Mrs Murphy. 'What will become of him? We shouldn't have brought him, Manfred. This safari is far too dangerous for a child like Max.'

'Let's stay calm, Millicent dear,' said Mr Murphy patting her with a trembling hand. 'I'm sure he'll be fine.'

The safari had trekked on after Max transformed, thinking he was with Molly at the back. Now they had stopped again to rest and discovered Max's disappearance.

'Molly, please go through it again. What exactly happened?' said Mr Ongondo.

'Well,' replied Molly, determined not to give away Max's secret, 'he was standing here and I think he went that way.' She pointed vaguely at the forest.

'But which way *exactly*?' asked Mr Murphy. 'What were his actual words before he left?'

'I think he . . . he . . . waaaah,' Molly sobbed and began rubbing her eyes. 'Will . . . will he be . . . all right?' she said, though she was actually thinking, *Really, I should be in Hollywood!*

Blubbing through her own tears, Mrs Murphy hugged her and said, 'There, there, poppet. We'll find him. I promise.' Mr Murphy pulled out a grubby handkerchief and gently dabbed Molly's face.

Mr Ongondo interrupted. 'Listen everybody. I'm afraid this situation is very serious. There are dozens of creatures out here that would love to tear out Max's throat, rip him to shreds and eat him.'

'Do you have to go into quite so much detail?' sobbed Mrs Murphy.

'You're right, Millicent,' said Mr Murphy, who had turned a sickly green. 'We should try to think positive.'

'If he's fortunate,' continued Mr Ongondo, 'he might survive until nightfall – but after dark he won't stand a chance. So we must hurry back to the lodge and raise the alarm.'

Professor Slynk, who had just switched off his walkie-talkie, interrupted.

'Let's not be hasty,' he said. 'He's a sensible lad and he's probably waiting nearby. You know how fond of him I am. I couldn't live with myself if anything bad happened, but in the time it takes to fetch help it might be too late! So I think we should stay here and make a careful search.'

'Professor!' said Mr Murphy. 'Could you radio back to base with your walkie-talkie and ask them to send urgent help?'

'No!' snapped Slynk. 'Sorry, I mean yes, . . . er . . . good idea, Manfred. Only . . . Oh! What a shame, the battery's just gone flat.'

Molly was watching Slynk through her fingers. *He's up to something and he's playing for time*, she thought. *He obviously doesn't want to go back, so that's got to be the best thing to do.*

'Actually,' said Molly loudly, 'I've just remembered. Max said he was hot and bored and his feet hurt and he was going back to the lodge.'

Slynk's plump, sweaty head turned crimson with rage. If he was forced back to the lodge he might lose contact with his men, but of course, he couldn't tell that to anyone. Molly looked him in the eye and gave her sweetest smile.

'No, that isn't possible!' said Mr Ongondo, who

as guide felt responsible for Max's safety. 'He couldn't just wander off.'

'It wouldn't be the first time,' said Mr Murphy.

'I said we must stay together. Wasn't he listening?' said Mr Ongondo.

'It would be just like Max,' said Mrs Murphy. 'He lives in a world of his own, and he was complaining dreadfully before we left.'

'If we don't find him soon he won't be complaining about anything at all!' said Mr Ongondo. 'There's no time to waste. We have to go back!'

'No!' said one of the other hikers, a tubby man in a baseball cap with large wet patches under his arms. 'I've saved up for years for this trip.'

'Me too,' spluttered another man, though it was hard to catch his words through his fuzzy ginger beard. 'Why should we spoil our trip because some ill-behaved brat won't follow the rules?'

'I agree,' squawked his wife. 'It'll teach him to do what he's told in future!'

'Not if he's dead, it won't!' snapped Mr Ongondo. Everyone looked shocked and stared at the ground. 'The rules still apply,' he continued. 'We'll all return to the lodge and we *must* stay together. If we're lucky, the Nairobi bus will be passing soon. So everyone, please head for the track.'

Coming towards them a dirty brown dust cloud grew slowly into a dirty brown bus that bucked and bounced across the savannah. Close up, Molly could see it was already crowded. A ladder on the back led to the roof, which was piled high with suitcases and furniture, rolled-up carpets and bicycles, baskets of chickens – even a cage full of goats.

Soon they were all aboard and the bus crawled away, carrying everyone, including a scowling Slynk, back to the lodge.

Meanwhile, Max lay in the grass watching Slynk's thugs. He covered his ears against the screeching and rattling from the cages near the lorry. He had to act quickly – the lions and hyenas were sure to hear soon and come looking for an easy meal. All but three of the strongest baboons had been caught, and they were running around the lorry barking and baring their teeth, flicking their eyelids to scare off Slynk's men.

Max ran across to the lorry and tried again to communicate: he jumped up and down, slapped his head, turned a somersault. He even did the chicken dance! No response. The baboons were so angry with the men they didn't notice him at all. The men did though.

'Look, there's another one.'

'What's it doing?'

'I don't know. Do you think it's the one the Professor wanted?'

'Yeah, let's get it!'

A net flicked straight towards him. Max ducked and another flew by, skimming his ear. He ran at the first man, but the net was ready to throw again and Max had to roll like a commando to save himself.

'That's him! That's him! I've never seen a monkey do that before!'

Before they could throw again Max shot between the two men and hopped behind one of the cages. *That was too close*, he thought. Max looked round, desperately thinking up another plan. Then his hand rested on a pile of rocks and he knew just what to do. He weighed up a pebble the size of a chocolate muffin and hurled it at one of Slynk's men, catching him sharply on the nose.

'Ow, wod's thad?' the man cried, clutching his face.

Max threw another that smacked the second man in the mouth, knocking out a couple of teeth.

'Argh!' he yelled as the other baboons got the idea and joined in, screeching merrily and flinging stones at the men.

Under the hail of pebbles and rocks, the men ran for the lorry. *No you don't*, thought Max, running towards them. Immediately, the other baboons joined in as Max leapt on the man with the bunch of keys hanging from his belt.

'Gerroff you hairy ape!' he yelled, punching and kicking as Max struggled to hold on and grab the keys.

Oi! I'm not an ape, thought Max. *I'm a baboon!*

Suddenly, another baboon landed on the man's head, blinding him with his large paws.

'Gnuck!' said Max without thinking.

'Gnuck!' said the new arrival with a nod. Max blinked in surprise and, seizing his chance, tugged the man's belt, snapping it and making his trousers fall down. Max snatched the keys and, yelping with joy, raced around unlocking all the cages.

Baboons swarmed out and mobbed the men as they staggered towards their lorry. Then, with one baboon still to free, Max heard the engine start. He couldn't leave the baboon in the cage . . . but the lorry was an easy way back to the lodge. And what about the film crew? He just couldn't think about them right now.

8. Softly, Softly, Catchee Monkey

The lorry shuddered and began to move. Max panicked and dropped the keys. *Stay calm and think!* said Max to himself. Quickly, he mimed throwing a stone at the truck. The troop understood immediately. Screeching and chattering with excitement, all baboons pelted the lorry with rocks.

Mirrors shattered, windows smashed and the driver zigzagged to avoid the barrage of stones.

Max slipped the key into the last padlock just as the lorry hit a fallen tree trunk and stalled. As the driver re-started the engine and reversed out, Max flung the cage door open then raced for the lorry, holding up a hand as he ran. Again, the baboons understood. They stopped throwing stones as Max sprang and landed with a bump on top of the cab.

The roof was as smooth as a baby baboon's bottom and, under the mid-day sun it was also hot enough to fry an egg. Max slithered about. The only place with a grip was the rim of the sunroof, so he lay flat on top of it clinging tight, biting his lip against the pain of the scorching metal.

Suddenly, the sunroof flew open and a head popped up through the hole, face to face with Max.

'Aghhh!' yelled the man through stumps of broken teeth. Terrified, his eyes rolling like marbles, he fell backwards into the cab.

Max howled with laughter as the lorry sped on, bumping and rattling across the savannah.

After his recent escapades, it seemed ages since he'd had such fun.

Up ahead Max saw another vehicle approaching. Straining to see clearly, he forgot to hold on and almost rolled off the cab! He just managed to grip the edge of the sunroof when it flew open again and the man appeared once more from the hole, an evil grin on his face. He held up a pointed stick.

'Hey monkey-face! How do you like this?' he shouted, jabbing Max with the stick.

'Grr!' growled Max, baring his teeth, but that just made the man angry – and he bared his gums back at Max! Stabbing and poking with the stick, he tried to topple Max off the lorry. Max dodged and ducked. He made a sudden grab and caught the stick, but lost his balance. He slipped off the roof and dangled over the side, clinging to the stick with one hand.

'Haa! Look at this,' the man called to the driver. 'I've been fishing and caught a monkey!' He shook the stick to make Max let go, but Max held on for his life, kicking and twisting until he got one foot on to the broken wing mirror and the other on to the door handle. He flicked out his tail, caught hold of the radio aerial with the other hand and, with just enough hold, he scrambled back on to the roof.

They started a tug-of-war with the stick, but with nothing to grip Max knew he was never going to win.

As they tugged and pulled, the cloud of dust from the other vehicle got closer, until Max saw it was the camera crew's safari truck. *Perfect timing! All change, please*, he thought. Knowing Max-the-boy couldn't judge a jump on to a moving target, he had to let his animal side take charge. It was getting easier now. Although he was still in the tug-of-war, he relaxed, breathed slowly and stopped thinking. A pleasant tingle ran through him, the sky turned a richer blue and again a thousand savannah scents filled his nostrils. The safari truck drew alongside and, with one lazy bound, Max let go of the stick, flew through the choking dust and landed softly on top of the truck.

As the dust settled Max took control again. Looking back he saw the lorry trundling into the distance and chuckled: Slynk's man was peering out of the sunroof in shock, wondering how the blue-eyed baboon had just disappeared into thin air!

For the first time since he had transformed Max sat quietly gazing at his surroundings. Early that morning the savannah had seemed boring. Soon afterwards, he discovered it was terrifying. Now, riding on the safari truck and enjoying the breeze riffling his fur, he thought it was beautiful - especially the view towards Mount Kilimanjaro.

He felt fond of the baboons and in awe of the lioness and leopard. *All the creatures have a place here, though. Except me, of course,* he thought, suddenly remembering a film he wanted to see very badly . . . the one with him in the starring role. He couldn't sit around all day dreaming. He had to get his hands on it!

This truck was far more comfortable than the lorry, with a luggage rail around the cab to stop him sliding off. It too had a sunroof. Using the end of his tail as a brush Max carefully flicked off the layer of dust and peered into the cab. Bill the cameraman was driving and chatting with Katie Plank, the presenter.

'I don't see why we have to go back,' said Bill. 'We'll never find that weird baboon again. And I don't fancy being stuck out here *all* Christmas Eve.'

'That's just it!' said Katie. 'That freak is out there somewhere. By tomorrow it *will* be long gone, but today . . . well, we might just strike lucky.' She patted the camera on the seat beside her. 'We have some amazing shots in here. With a little more, we could fill a whole documentary!'

'But –'

'No buts, Bill. Imagine!' said Katie spreading her arms wide. 'Instead of a brief mention at the end there'll be my . . . er, our names on the title credits!'

'I'd bet my mum's wig we never see it again,' said Bill.

Max had heard enough insults for one day and decided it was time to act. He wouldn't get a better chance to snatch that film. First, he teased his fingers under the edge of the sunroof. Then, each time the truck lurched over a bump, he heaved it up a little further. After a few minutes he had an opening big enough to squeeze his arm through. *Lucky I didn't turn into an elephant after all*, he thought. *If I'd jumped up here, I'd have squashed them! Though with a trunk it would've been much easier to reach the camera.*

Slowly, silently he eased an arm through the gap, worrying that if Bill saw something big and hairy dangling in his cab he might crash the truck with the shock – and luggage racks didn't come with seat belts.

Despite his extra-long baboon arms Max could barely reach. He stretched his fingers until they ached, and just managed to touch the eject button.

The tape popped out! Katie heard a noise and shot her hand out, grabbing the tape first. Max snatched it back and whipped his arm up through the roof. He clamped the tape between his teeth, hurled himself from the roof and bounded away at top speed.

'Nooooo! Stop! Thief! That's mine!' shrieked Katie.

Bill spun the truck into a screaming handbrake turn, spewing a huge dust cloud into the air.

'Quick! Quick! He's getting away!' Katie wailed.

'Not if I can help it!' muttered Bill and he slammed the accelerator pedal to the floor.

9. The Wheels On the Bus

Max raced through the grass kicking up a dust trail of his own. He urgently needed a break, just two minutes to shred the tape. He paused in a hollow, but in a moment the truck roared up behind him. He hid in a bush – a second later they flushed him out. Escaping from lions, leopards and charging buffalo had not been easy, but compared to fooling an angry film crew with two sets of eyes and go-anywhere wheels it was a piece of cake.

Looking around the wide savannah, Max

knew the other animals couldn't help. This time he was on his own, and the only way out was by going back into the forest.

The truck powered towards him again.

'There! There! Run it down. I want that film!' shrilled Katie above the growling engine.

This time Max deliberately relaxed and felt the tingle spread through him. The hum of insects rose above the thundering truck, leaves on the acacia trees shimmered emerald and, as the truck zoomed by, he skipped easily to one side. Before they could turn round he shot away, fleeing for the woods, enjoying again the thrill of speeding through the grass with the wind in his fur. The tape gripped between his teeth made breathing difficult, but now he was nearly there – over the track and the clearing, and he'd be safe. In fact, he seemed to have lost them already – but he wasn't taking any chances.

Without looking, Max ran across the road. 'Honk! Honk!' bellowed a horn. He sprang aside just in time as the great black wheels of a bus thundered past, missing him by a whisker and spraying him with dirt. The shock snapped the animal spell and made him think as a boy again. He'd been concentrating so hard on reaching the trees he hadn't seen the bus coming. Now it trundled away, crammed with passengers, piled high with luggage ... and there, staring out of the window was a worried-looking Molly! Max waved wildly, but she didn't see him.

Wait for me! he thought, and he gave chase, choking in the dust spraying from the bus wheels. *At least the dust will hide me from the film crew,* Max coughed.

Though it was old and slow, the bus was still a moving target. Each time Max got close it lurched and, missing the ladder, he fell on his face. *I need help*, he thought. Then he suddenly realised it was there already, inside him. All the help he needed just waiting to be let out.

It didn't matter that he was still chasing the bus, he started to relax and straight away, much stronger than before, the warm tingle surged through him, washing all the way to the end of his tail. The rickety bus now seemed to roll smoothly, gliding over bumps. Together, he and it became like two boats rising and falling with the tide. Slowly, he caught up and with one powerful leap, grasped the ladder and scrambled quickly on to the roof.

Immediately the tingle left him, and the bus rocked and jolted alarmingly. One big bump threw him almost over the edge. He grabbed the luggage rack with both feet and held tight. With one hand he clutched a crate of squawking hens, then he wrapped his tail round the leg of a white-painted wicker chair.

Max dropped the film and lay low on a suitcase, gasping mouthfuls of clean air and spitting dirt from his teeth. Suddenly the film truck came in view again. Bill, mad at losing the tape, was driving the truck round in crazy circles. They definitely hadn't spotted Max! Bouncing over tussocks at break-neck speed the safari truck faded slowly into the horizon and Max breathed a sigh of relief. At last he could destroy the film.

His jaws ached from clenching the box for so long, but they were still strong. A crunch and a crack with his great fangs and the case disintegrated. *That was so easy*, Max chuckled to himself. Then he bit the tape and . . . oh dear! It was like giant dental floss. It curled round his teeth, but wouldn't snap. It twisted itself into a ball, but didn't break. He knew he had to shred it – just smashing the case wasn't enough. If only he had a knife! He looked around. *There might be one in the suitcase*, Max thought, then he shook his head. Taking something from someone else's luggage felt very wrong. Then *eureka*! He had an idea.

Holding a splinter of the shattered video case in his teeth, he slashed it across the tape. Success! He did it again and a shiny strip fluttered in the wind then blew away, lost in the wide savannah. *Now I'm a litterbug*, he thought. *Would adding something to someone's luggage be OK? Definitely better than leaving rubbish all over the park and harming the animals!*

He worked quickly, shredding the tape and cramming it into different bags, thinking, *Is this the part where I rescued the piglet?* or, *Maybe this is the bit where I danced? Either way, Katie Plank won't be seeing it again.*

The bus shook and bounced. Max was so busy slicing up the film he didn't notice as, little by little, the wicker chair held by his tail wobbled towards the edge. Then, with a sudden crash, the

chair toppled over the side of the bus and dangled from his tail! The noise upset the hens and goats, which began clucking and bleating.

'Stop the bus!' someone yelled from inside, seeing the tail and thinking a baboon was trying to eat their chickens.

'My goats! It's after my goats!' shrieked another voice.

'Can't stop,' shouted the driver. 'We're hurrying back for the rescue team.'

The chair kept bumping against the window. Max was worried it might smash the glass, but couldn't let go of it – it belonged to someone on the bus. He tried to pull it up but someone leaned out of the window and tugged it.

'Eeeek!' he yelped, and he slipped right over the edge. He scrabbled frantically and caught hold of the luggage rail. Then began his third tug-of-war in one day: he heaved himself up . . . grasping

hands snatched the chair away, then grabbed his tail. He pulled up . . . they tugged down. He pulled harder . . . they tugged harder still.

His tail started tingling . . . *No! No! Any time but now!* Max knew that tingle – he was changing back. In two minutes he'd be a boy again. They'd see him transform right in front of them!

His arms were shrinking, getting weaker by the second. His face hurt like he'd walked into a lamp post. Sweat dripped from every pore, his skin prickled all over. Then, like a pinging elastic band, his tail slipped through the grappling hands of the passengers and shot back into his bottom. The stinging pain from the leopard's gash disappeared with the tail and with a last mighty heave he landed with a thump on the roof. Wedged between a suitcase and the goat cage he squealed as his fur melted like burning wax into his skin. His eyes swelled and popped back into the front of his face with a squishy 'plop'. With a 'shhlurp' his fangs slid back into his gums. Breathing heavily he patted himself all over. Yes, he was Max again. Two arms . . . two legs . . . slightly podgy belly and . . . naked . . . *naked*!

'Arghh!'

He knew it was wrong. He knew it was bad . . . but he *had* to open someone's suitcase and find something to wear.

10. The Naked Truth

*O*ops! thought Max, tripping over a box of pineapples. *Lucky that film crew can't see this.*

With every jolt of the bus he fell, sprawling among the luggage – balancing had been so much easier as a baboon. He lay on his side and opened the first case. Slivers of film fluttered in the wind, but it contained only bundles of baby clothes. He tried another case. Cuddly toys. He crawled along the roof and tried another – towelling nappies!

'Ow!' he muttered, as a chicken pecked his ear. *It can't be true!* he thought. He'd checked every box, bag and case on the bus but found nothing he could wear – unless you counted nappies.

'Noooo,' he groaned aloud. 'I can't!' But when it comes down to a choice between naked or nappies, there's only one answer! A goat poked its head through the bars of its cage and nibbled his toes as Max tied four nappies together into a clumsy skirt and slipped it on.

He stood up. The bus lurched. He wobbled. He slipped. He fell over the edge!

'Help!' he squeaked, grabbing the luggage bar again. Only this time his human hands were weak and sweaty. Immediately the bar started slipping through his fingers. He snatched hold of a luggage strap, but his arms couldn't take his weight.

'Help!' he shouted again, as his world tumbled into slow motion.

I'm going to die! he thought, knowing that he'd either break his neck and get eaten by scavengers, or survive the fall only to be eaten by predators. *And I don't want to miss Christmas.*

Suddenly, he jerked to a stop. Hands grabbed his legs and dragged him through the bus window!

'Thanks –' Max started to say, but turning round he couldn't believe his eyes. Round spectacles. Blubbery lips. Wispy black hair. A sweaty, babyish face. It was *Stink!*

'Say it then,' growled Slynk. 'Tell me how grateful you are that I saved your worthless little life.'

'What do you mean, worthless?' said Max playing for time. He really was grateful, it was just hard to say the words. Why, out of everyone on the bus, did it have to be Slynk? He looked round, trying to see his family. He knew Molly was on the bus, so Dad and Mum were sure to be there too. But where? He couldn't see them through the crowd of passengers who were now staring at him, smirking at his nappy skirt.

Slynk hadn't noticed what Max was wearing. He was too busy rummaging in his medical kit.

'Here it is,' he muttered, and with a thin smile of satisfaction, he pulled a bottle from the bag. On the label, below a skull and crossbones, was one word: 'Chloroform'.

'What's that?' said Max suspiciously, as Slynk struggled to unscrew the safety cap from the bottle.

'Ah, just something to make you feel better!' said Slynk.

'What, like your little green tablets?' said Max trying to back away. 'No thanks!'

'I've got you now,' Slynk whispered. 'So don't make a scene. I promise you won't feel a thing.'

Suddenly, he heard Molly calling. 'Max! Max!'

'Over here!' he called back, and a moment later she burst through the crush of passengers.

'Molly!' said Max. 'Am I glad to see you!'

'No!' groaned Slynk. 'Get lost you little squirt. He's mine now.'

'Never!' said Molly, dragging Max back through the bus. 'Come on, Max. Let's get away from *Stink!*'

'Phew! That was a close one, Molly, but how did you know to come? I looked around but couldn't see you anywhere.'

'I've no idea, Max. I just had a feeling you were in danger, like when you know it's dinner-time without looking at the clock. Perhaps it's a twin thing?'

'Anyway,' she continued with a chuckle, 'what on earth are you doing wearing a skirt? Or is it a nappy?'

'It's not a skirt or a nappy – it's a kilt.'

'OK, keep your hair on.'

'Anyway, forget about that,' Max said. Then he whispered, 'Little sis, did you get my clothes?'

'Clothes?' said Molly with a puzzled grin. 'Let me think.'

'You have! Where are they?'

'Umm?'

'All right, you're not *little* sis. I'm sorry.'

'And you won't call me "little" ever again?'

'No. Now where are they?'

'Promise?'

'OK. I promise . . .' said Max, crossing his fingers behind his back.

'They're in my bag under the seat.'

'. . . not,' said Max gleefully, uncrossing his fingers, then he suddenly gave Molly a shove. 'Quick, Stink's coming!'

They were jostling along the aisle when someone screamed.

'My baby!'

Oh, no! Max thought. *It's Mum. Now I've got some explaining to do.*

Mrs Murphy charged through the crowd like an ice-breaker, grabbed Max and hugged him tightly, saying over and over, 'My baby, oh, my baby.'

Mr Murphy followed his wife and stood patting Max on the shoulder, tears of relief in his eyes.

Then Slynk arrived and saved Max again, this time from an embarrassing scene.

'Millicent, Manfred, you've found him. I'm *so* glad he's OK,' he said as though he'd eaten a whole jar of smarmalade. 'Did you know I saved him?'

'Preston, how can we ever thank you?' said Mrs Murphy.

'Oh, it was nothing,' said Slynk. 'Max was larking about up on the roof, and fell off. He could have died, but I caught him. I was so relieved. I couldn't bear it if he came to any harm.'

Max couldn't believe his ears – Stink was such a liar!

'Ma-ax,' said Mrs Murphy frowning. 'Is this true?'

'Um . . .' Max mumbled staring at the floor. In two seconds, Dad and Mum had changed from weepy worried parents to smoking human volcanoes just about to blow. He hated to give Slynk any credit, but what else could he do? He nodded.

'Did you stop to think about anyone else?' said Dad.

Max shook his head.

'You've had us worried sick!' said Mum.

'Sorry,' he mumbled.

'You've spoilt the safari for everyone!' said Dad. 'Now tell us exactly what happened?'

Max fiddled with his fingers and couldn't look anyone in the eye. 'I, um . . . well, my feet were sore and I sat down for a rest, but you all carried on. I tried to catch up but got lost. I looked everywhere, but couldn't find you.'

He stared out of the window as if remembering the trauma, but actually trying to think of what to say next. 'Er . . . then I heard something growling and thought it might eat me,' he looked up at Mrs Murphy with wide eyes. *Hey, I'm good at this*, he thought, seeing the worried look return to her face.

'Then I saw the bus,' he continued, 'but I didn't have any money for a ticket, so I climbed up with the luggage. Then I felt so tired I fell asleep.'

'And what *are* you wearing? It looks like a nappy,' said Mum.

'It's a kilt!' said Max. 'I woke up so hot I had to take my clothes off. Then I fell asleep again and a goat ate them.'

Molly nudged him and shook her head – this was starting to sound ridiculous, but Max carried on.

'Then I found this *kilt* on the roof. I was just putting it on when I slipped and fell off the roof. Then kind Professor Slynk saved me.'

'Ahhh, my brave boy,' said Mrs Murphy with a fond smile.

Max grinned at Molly and whispered, 'Dad was right. I really have had the experience of a lifetime. It was a fantastic adventure. I can't wait to tell you about it.'

'Yeah,' said Molly, holding her nose. 'And we'll have all Christmas to talk about it, but first, you need a bath.'

More Marvellous Monkey Facts!

They're spiritual creatures! The ancient Egyptians thought that the baboon was a sacred animal and used to worship it.

They're marmo-pets! Back in the eighteenth century, people in England and America kept monkeys – particularly marmosets – as pets. They dressed them up in tiny clothes and when the monkeys died their owners would stuff them and put them on display. Ewww!

They're spies! During the Napoleonic war a shipwreck landed on the British coastline. The locals believed the only surviving crew member (a monkey) to be a spy. A trial was held but with the primate unable to answer questions the poor animal was sentenced to death!

They've got comfy seats! Though baboons are hairy, their bottoms are bald with a built-in cushion called a callus.

They're party animals! Baboons are social creatures and live in groups. A small group may only have five members, but a large one may contain up to 250 members!

They like a snack! Like hamsters, baboons have pouches in their cheeks where they store food so that they can bring them out later when they fancy a snack!

ONLY JOKING!

What's sweet, white and fluffy and swings through the trees?

Meringue-utans!

Why don't humans like monkey menus?

Because they're totally bananas!

What do you call a monkey who talks too much?

A hot air baboon!

Are You a Monkey?

According to Chinese astrology, there's an animal inside all of us, trying to get out. Look up the year you were born on the chart below and find out just how beastly you are. And discover how well you get on with the 'monkeys' in your life.

YEAR OF BIRTH	SIGN:
1949, 1961, 1973, 1985 or 1997	OX
1950, 1962, 1974, 1986 or 1998	TIGER
1951, 1963, 1975, 1987 or 1999	RABBIT
1952, 1964, 1976, 1988 or 2000	DRAGON
1953, 1965, 1977, 1989 or 2001	SNAKE
1954, 1966, 1978, 1990 or 2002	HORSE
1955, 1967, 1979, 1991 or 2003	SHEEP
1956, 1968, 1980, 1992 or 2004	MONKEY
1957, 1969, 1981, 1993 or 2005	ROOSTER
1958, 1970, 1982, 1994 or 2006	DOG
1959, 1971, 1983, 1995 or 2007	PIG
1960, 1972, 1984, 1996 or 2008	RAT

Now you've found out which animal you are, read on to discover what it all means . . .

OX: You're great because . . . you're reliable, determined and hard-working.
How do Oxen get on with Monkeys?
It's a miracle if you get on, as you don't have that much in common. Monkeys are just too crazy for you!

TIGER: You're great because . . . you're brave, confident and imaginative.
How do Tigers get on with Monkeys?
Your personalities are strong and although you're likely to have a few falling outs, you do like each other

RABBIT: You're great because . . . you're friendly, tactful and sensitive.
How do Rabbits get on with Monkeys?
Rabbits like loyalty and the Monkey's quite selfish. It's not likely that you two would get on too well

DRAGON: You're great because . . . you're attractive, romantic and generous.
How do Dragons get on with Monkeys?
Extremely well! With your originality and the Monkey's wit, you're a compatible and popular pair!

SNAKE: You're great because . . . you're good-looking, deep and charismatic. **How do Snakes get on with Monkeys?** The Monkey could take advantage of you, making the chances of a lasting friendship very slim

HORSE: You're great because . . . you're practical, independent and strong.
How do Horses get on with Monkeys?
You both try very hard to get on, but for some reason it just never seems to happen

SHEEP: You're great because . . . you're gentle, clever and fun-loving.
How do Sheep get on with Monkeys?
You're both sociable, have a good understanding of each other and enjoy each other's company

MONKEY: You're great because . . . you're intelligent, quick-thinking and adventurous.
How do two Monkeys get on together?
You're a bit too competitive to be best buddies

ROOSTER: You're great because . . . you're self-assured, honest and straight-talking.
How do Roosters get on with Monkeys?
You're too demanding for the meek little Monkey – could be a tricky friendship

DOG: You're great because . . . you're loyal, trustworthy and fair.
How do Dogs get on with Monkeys?
You're a great influence on the cheeky Monkey and could even get them to behave themselves!

PIG: You're great because . . . you're outgoing, well-organised and big-hearted.
How do Pigs get on with Monkeys?
This is the best friendship ever! Together you'll always have a great time and a whole load of laughs

RAT: You're great because . . . you're charming, warm-hearted and passionate.
How do Rats get on with Monkeys?
Brilliantly! You have a top friendship, with loads in common, especially your love of gossip!

UNCLE HERBERT'S MONKEY-FACE SANDWICHES

Uncle Herbert could munch on these all day, so keep an eye on your cheeky little sarnies! This recipe serves eight

YOU'LL NEED:

16 slices of brown bread

8 slices of ham

Pickle or mayonnaise – whichever you prefer

8 slices of cheese

A handful of raisins

A chopping board

A 7-centimetre biscuit cutter

A grown-up helper

HERE'S WHAT TO DO:

1. Cut out 16 circles of brown bread, using the biscuit cutter. Do this on the chopping board so you don't make marks on the kitchen worktop!

2. Make more circles from the sliced ham and the cheese slices. Keep the scraps

3. Lay out eight of your bread circles and spread lightly with pickle or mayonnaise

4. Top each of the eight circles of bread with a layer of ham and a layer of cheese

5. Complete the sandwiches by placing the other eight bread circles on top of the bases

6. Make the monkey faces using the raisins and make ears out of the scraps of bread, ham and cheese

CHEEKY!

Can't wait for the next book
in the series?
Here's a sneak preview of

available now from all good bookshops, or
www.beastlybooks.com

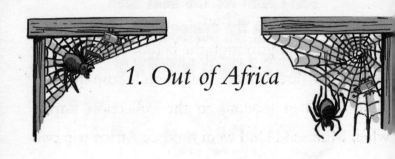

1. Out of Africa

'**B**reakfast special!' Uncle Herbert yelled up the stairs. 'Come and get it!'

'Oh, no,' groaned Max, hiding under his quilt. 'That's all I need.'

Molly knocked on his bedroom door, 'Hurry up, Max. It might be something interesting.'

'I'd just like something normal,' he muttered, then shouted. 'I'll be down in five minutes.' He crawled out of bed and started his morning routine:

- Stare blearily into the mirror and pat down cockatoo-like tufts of hair
- Clear a path through the bedroom by pushing yesterday's dirty plates, mugs and crisp packets under the bed (adding to the collection started when Mum and Dad went on their Africa trip two weeks ago)
- Rummage through the jumble on the floor and rescue all socks
- Yawn like a hippo while putting on the freshest socks from the pile
- Repeat as above for pants, shirt and trousers
- Search under bed for games console and through jumble of clothes for last week's history homework – due in yesterday!
- Empty sweet wrappers and comics from school bag. Cram crumpled history homework (plus fresh supply of crisps and chocolate biscuits) into bag

• Drag bag downstairs and dump it in the middle of the hall

• Shuffle into the kitchen and collapse, exhausted, on to a chair

With Mum and Dad away, making breakfast was the job of Uncle Herbert, whose taste buds came from a charity shop on Planet Weird. Last week he had served up chicken drumsticks in custard, mackerel and trifle pie, and then strawberry tikka masala with gravy.

'D'you mind if I just have cereal today, Uncle Herbert?' asked Max.

'If you like, Max. Before you decide, however, I should mention that I've made my "Monday Special", so you may change your mind.'

'Really?' said Max suspiciously. 'What's that?'

'Guess!' teased his uncle. 'Here's a clue: put the darkest thing next to water with an "a" not an "e", add a fish – but not a red one – and cook in a case.'

'That's easy!' said Molly, who'd seen the empty packets in the bin . . . and chosen cornflakes. 'Come on, Max.'

Max stared at the ceiling for a while, then said, 'I'm really sorry, Uncle Herbert, but I can't think. I've got two zillion tests coming up and I can't concentrate on anything else.'

'Except playing very important computer games all night,' snorted Molly.

'But that's for relaxation, *after* I've done my revision!'

Uncle Herbert started whistling and Max looked up, pleased to change the subject. 'Is that a clue?'

Still whistling, Uncle Herbert nodded.

'Um . . . song . . . long . . . spaghetti?' suggested Max.

Uncle Herbert shook his head.

'Song . . . tune . . . tuna! Something with tuna?'

'No!' said Molly, as Uncle Herbert mimed

switching off the light, then digging a hole. 'The whistling was a red herring – get it?'

'Switch . . . itch . . . pepper?'

Again, Uncle Herbert shook his head.

'Light . . . delight . . . Turkish delight?'

'Pathetic!' said Molly. 'It's sooo simple. The darkest thing is black. Put it next to water with an "e" not an "a" equals *blackcurrant*. Add a fish – but not a red one – is *herring*. Cook in a case equals *pie. So,* it's blackcurrant and herring pie, isn't it, Uncle?' Molly preened herself.

'Well done, Molly!' smiled Uncle Herbert tucking into a large bowlful. 'Mmm, this is good! Help yourself, Max.'

'Er . . . I'm not very hungry this morning,' said Max. 'I think I'll just have cornflakes.'

As Max poured his milk the doorbell rang. Uncle Herbert left the table to answer it.

'Molly,' whispered Max. 'I *really* need some help. Can you do my English essay for me? It's just that I've got all these tests coming up and I've got behind with my French, history and science.'

Molly folded her arms and tilted her head, just like Mum. 'Is that all?'

'Oh, yes. I forgot. Maths.'

'And . . .?'

'And geography.'

'Have you noticed,' said Molly, 'that, being the same age –'

'*Nearly* the same age,' said Max. 'I'm ten

minutes older, remember?'

Molly ignored the taunt. 'As I was saying, being the same age, we both get exactly the same work. So how come I'm bang up to date and you're so . . . useless?'

'I am *not!*'

Molly raised her eyebrows. 'Computer games. Need I say more?'

'It's not my fault. It's the games companies. They keep bringing out new levels. If I stopped playing I'd lose my ranking.'

'I do your homework so you can play games? I don't think so. There's an easy answer – concentrate on your schoolwork.'

'You sound just like Mum. Anyway, it's not the games. It's the animal transformations. They keep happening and I can't stop thinking about it. Please help me, Molly. If you don't I'll do really badly in all the tests.

'OK,' said Molly. 'But only if you unplug that computer!'

Max was about to protest when the kitchen door shuddered and Uncle Herbert's voice mumbled from the other side, 'Ah, yes! Always a good idea to open it first.'

Then in came an enormous parcel covered in stickers that said, 'Fragile,' and 'This Way up'. It was followed into the room by Uncle Herbert.

'It's from Africa and addressed to you two,' he said. 'It must be from your Mum and Dad!' He dropped it on the floor and went back in the hall to sign the delivery slip.

The twins rushed over and ripped open the box. They started pulling out handfuls of straw padding and trying to guess what might be inside.

'Huh!' said Max, holding up a piece of bright red-and-yellow cloth. 'A tea towel? What's the point? I never do the drying up.'

'Maybe that *is* the point!' laughed Molly.

'This looks better,' he said picking up a small statue of a man with a tooth necklace and a sharp bone through his nose. It reminded him of the village healer he'd met the first time he'd transformed.

'This is cool,' he said. Then in a hopeful whisper he added, 'Hey, Molly. Do you think this might be

to help me control the transformations?'

'No. How could it be? Mum and Dad don't know about them, do they?'

Max felt disappointed, but continued emptying the box. He looked at the growing pile of bead bracelets, shell necklaces and carved animals. There were even shakers like the maracas they had at primary school.

'This is all rubbish! Why on earth did Mum and Dad think we'd want this heap of junk?'

Molly reached to the bottom of the box. 'Hold on! This looks interesting.'

'Oh, yeah?'

'No, really. Look!' said Molly, lifting out a face mask carved from dark rosewood. It had empty, cut-out eyes and real human teeth that stuck up like crooked tombstones. It was painted all over with white spots and red lines, and from the chin hung a beard made of animal hair.

'Wow! That's *scary*!' said Max.

'It's like the ones we've been studying in art. I'll take it to school – maybe we could draw it in still life.'

'It'd be better than a boring bowl of fruit,' said Max.

Just as Molly shoved the mask into her bag Max saw one of the eyes move! *But it couldn't*, he thought. *They're just holes*. He stepped back, pointing at Molly's bag.

'Er . . . Molly. I think −' he began. Then the doorbell rang again suddenly.

'Your friend Jake's here,' called Uncle Herbert.

Max and Molly grabbed their bags and soon all three of them were chatting and walking up the road to school.

'What were you saying earlier, Max?' asked Molly as they turned the corner at the end of the road.

'Saying? When?'

'Just before Jake arrived.'

'Um . . . I don't remember,' said Max. 'It can't have been anything important.'

But inside Molly's bag something really was moving and it wasn't going to help Max's schoolwork at all.